Exploring National Parks

Robin C. Fitzsimmons

Contents

Rigby

Exploring National Parks

Do you live near a park? Do you walk your dog or ride your bike there?

Would you like to visit a park where alligators swim?

What about a park where steam rises from the ground and shoots into the air?

Come along and visit some of the national parks in our country.

Think of times you've gone to a park. What did you see? What did you hear? How did you feel?

A National Park in Florida

You'll need a boat if you want to travel through Everglades National Park. It is a large **swamp.** There are strange and beautiful sights to see in the Everglades.

The Everglades is home to many kinds of animals. Can you spot the alligators in the above picture? What other animals might live in the Everglades?

What do you imagine as you read about the Everglades?

A National Park in Colorado

The Dinosaur National **Monument** is in a pit of sand and rock. It was once home to many dinosaurs. Many years ago there was a river in the pit. Sometimes the river flooded.

The bones of dead dinosaurs were buried under mud and sand. After a long time, the mud, sand, and bones turned to rock.

What do you think dinosaur bones feel like?

A National Park in Wyoming

At Yellowstone National Park you can see Old Faithful. Old Faithful is a **geyser.** It shoots hot water and steam high into the air.

Yellowstone was the first national park in the United States. Besides geysers, there are hot springs, forests, and cliffs. Many kinds of wildlife live there.

Think of different times you've seen steam. What did it look like? How did it sound?

A National Park in Alaska

Watch an eagle fly. See a whale leap out of the water. Listen to a wolf howl. Many different animals call **Glacier** Bay National Park their home.

CRACK! That is the sound of ice crashing into the bay. Big pieces of ice called glaciers cover the mountains. Sometimes, pieces of a glacier break off and crash into the bay.

Think of times you've heard ice fall. How did it sound?

A National Park in Hawaii

The earth begins to shake. You look up. Hot smoke, ash, and melted rock shoot out the top of a mountain. It's a **volcano.**

You are in Volcanoes National Park.
The largest volcano in the world is here,
and it's erupting!

Imagine what
it might feel like to have
the earth rumble
beneath your feet.

The National Park Service

There are many national parks in the United States. The National Park Service takes care of the parks and takes visitors on park tours.

The pictures on the National Park Service's sign have special meanings. The tree and the buffalo stand for plants and animals. The mountains and the water stand for beauty and fun.

What images did you make in your head as you read about the national parks? How did they help you as you read?

NATIONAL PARK SERVICE

Department of the Interior

Wrap It Up

Use your senses to create images about the national parks.

- smoke
- hot rock
- ash

smell

- earth rumble

feel

- smoke in air

taste

Volcanoes National Park

see

hear

- smoke
- burning land
- Boom!

Picture yourself at a national park. What would you see, hear, smell, feel, taste?